MW00892550

Weldon Wexford & MURKLE MONSTER

by David Ezra Spinner

pictures by Peggy Collins

For all those who are humble dreamers. May your curiosity, creativity, and kindness lead you on the extra-ordinarily-magic-tastically best adventure of your life!
-David Ezra Spinner

weldonandmurkle@gmail.com.

weldonandmurkle.com

Illustration and design by Peggy Collins

ISBN 978-0-9863085-0-5
Second Edition

Here is my wizard family.

Extraordinarily BORING.

But not me!
I'm extra-ordinarily-magic-tastically fun!

I find adventures around the house. My parents find chores around the house.

I eat a bowl of jellybeans for dinner. They eat a bowl of beets. YUCK!

I am BORED.

My
EXTRA-ORDINARILY-MAGIC-TASTICALLY
imagination has gone BLANK.

What will my next adventure be?

I fly around the house on my broom
and think really hard.

I've changed my bed
into a pirate ship.
I've even turned my living
room into a castle.

I ask the gnomes in the garden
for a suggestion...
but they are busy working.

And then a lightning bolt goes
off in my head.

THAT'S IT!

I am ready for **my very own monster.**

I beg and beg my parents for a monster. I even **PROMISE** to eat **beets.**

"Monsters are a lot of work," says my dad. "Are you ready for that?" asks my mom.

"I am READY!"
My parents and I make a
magical deal.

So we fly on our dragon
to the Monster Shop.

I'm extra-ordinarily-
magic-tastically excited!

I look for the perfect monster.
They are all different shapes and sizes.

I see a monster zip overhead.
He is exploring the shop in a flying machine.

He is extra-ordinarily-magic-tastically curious.

"That's the one!"

I name him MURKLE MONSTER.

We become best friends.

This is going to be the best
adventure EVER!

My parents make a list for me...

Taking care of MONSTER list:

1. Visit Monster Vet
2. Buy a monster collar
3. Buy monster Bits
4. Take monster for walks
5. Make Monster Bed
6. Clean up monster poop.
7. Give monster bath

I go through the list one by one.

We take Murkle Monster for a check up.

"His heart is **ROARING** perfectly," says the doctor.

I find him a
monster collar.
And even
GOGGLES
like mine.

So far, taking care of a monster is **extra-ordinarily-magic-tastically** easy. But Monster poop is stinky.

Murkle Monster has A LOT
of energy.
So we suit up for some exercise.

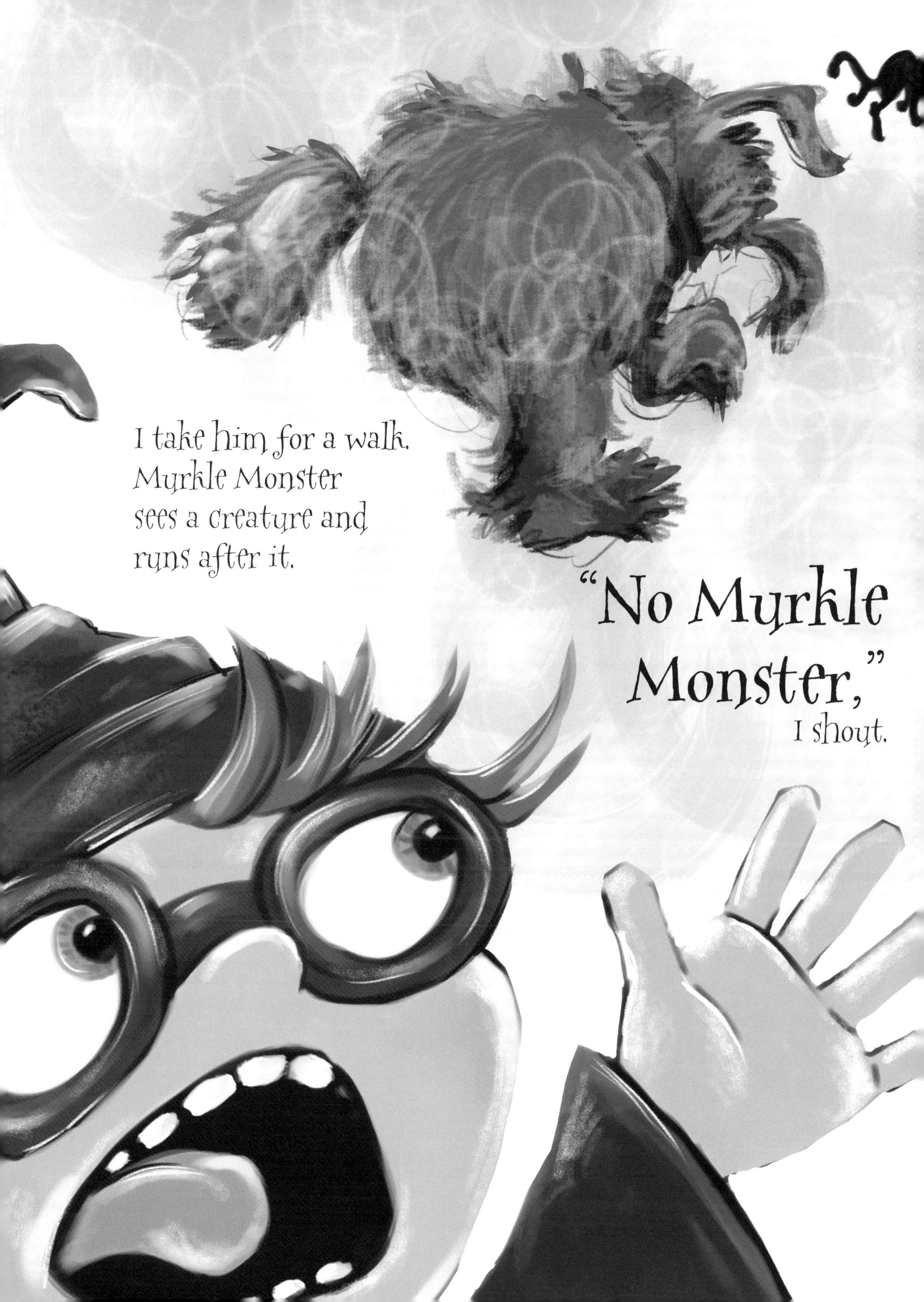

I take him for a walk.
Murkle Monster
sees a creature and
runs after it.

"No Murkle
Monster,"
I shout.

"Time for dinner," says mom.
I pour myself jellybeans and even some beets. Murkle Monster gets monster bits.

I wash my hands before I eat.
When I get back Murkle Monster has eaten everything EXCEPT the beets.

"NO MURKLE MONSTER," I shout.

I make a bed for
Murkle Monster.

"That's where
you'll sleep."

Murkle Monster howls all night.

"No Murkle Monster," I say.

Murkle Monster digs holes all over the yard.

The gnomes are FURIOUS.
My parents are FURIOUS.

Murkle Monster is out of control.

"No Murkle Monster,"
"No Murkle Monster,"
"NO MURKLE
MONSTER!!!"

"This list is EXTRA-ORDINARILY - MAGIC-TASTICALLY hard."

Maybe I'm not ready for a monster.

Murkle Monster **refuses** to take a bath.

He grabs my wand and
changes it into a
SWAMP.

And then a lightning bolt goes
off in my head.

THAT'S IT!

I go to the library and read
about monsters.
I learn so much.

I buy Murkle Monster his very own monster toys.

And **train** him with monster treats.

I **reward** him when he listens.

I teach Murkle
Monster some spells.

He even teaches me.

We all go on an

ADVENTURE

together.

Here is my wizard family now.

EXTRA-ORDINARILY-MAGIC-TASTICALLY MAGICAL!

CPSIA information can be obtained at www.ICGtesting.com
Printed in the USA
LVIW01n2349260315
432195LV00002B/2